ISBN 0-590-64755-5

Text copyright © 1997 by Rosemary Wells.
Illustrations copyright © 1997 by Susan Jeffers.
All rights reserved. Published by Scholastic Inc., 555 Broadway, New York, NY 10012,
by arrangement with Hyperion Books for Children.

SCHOLASTIC and associated logos are trademarks and/or registered
trademarks of Scholastic Inc.

12 11 10 9 8 7 6 5 4 3 2 1   8 9/9 0 1 2 3/0

Printed in the U.S.A.   14

First Scholastic printing, March 1998

Rosemary Wells
McDuff Comes Home

PICTURES BY Susan Jeffers

SCHOLASTIC INC.
New York Toronto London Auckland Sydney

McDuff's corner of the garden was just under the kitchen where he could hear the voices of the people he loved.

There McDuff relaxed and breathed in all the wonderful smells that escaped from the window . . . the snappy smell of Fred's frying sausages, the velvety smell of Lucy's vanilla rice pudding.

One day the window was closed.
There was nothing to smell or hear.

Suddenly, McDuff saw something move in the neighbor's garden.

It was a fat rabbit.

Zoom! went the rabbit through the zinnias.
McDuff squeezed through the fence after it.

His collar and tag caught on the fence.
Snap! went his collar and it fell off behind him.

The rabbit zigzagged over the neighbor's lawn
and whizzed across the street.

McDuff zigzagged and whizzed, too.

Over hills and streets and flower beds, the rabbit scurried and skedaddled with McDuff right on his tail until it found a hole and shot in. McDuff could not follow.

McDuff was so tired from chasing the rabbit that he lay down in someone's vegetable garden and fell asleep.

When McDuff woke up, he looked around.
He could not see his kitchen window.

He could not smell sausages or vanilla rice pudding.
He could not hear any voices he knew.

Mrs. Higgins came out to weed her garden.
"Who's that under my eggplants?" she asked.

Mrs. Higgins looked for McDuff's collar and tag and could not find them. "We will go to the police station," she said, "and see if anyone is there to pick you up."

Mrs. Higgins drove McDuff up Main Street and down Pine Road and over the bridge to Oak Lane. Suddenly McDuff smelled vanilla rice pudding.

"Woof," said McDuff. Mrs. Higgins turned left.
Then McDuff heard someone he loved calling his name.
"Woof," said McDuff. She turned right.

Then he saw his own house at Number Seven Elm Road.
Lucy and Fred were calling for him.
"Woof woof!" he said, and Mrs. Higgins stopped.

"His collar is gone!" said Lucy. "How did you know
where to bring him?"
"I guess I understand dog language," she said.

Everyone was hungry.
Lucy made some apple pie and sandwiches.

Fred gave McDuff his favorite treat, a small dish of vanilla rice pudding with a sausage sliced on top.